PRAISE FOR *LOST THINGS*

"A recycled skeleton seeing stars for the first time. A Greek god at a music festival. Our 'sedimentary insides.' Sam Haviland's poems are all of these things and more—'lost things' found and allowed to shine in their sidelong beauty, indexed until the image bursts through the line. 'The sun *is* a star,' Haviland reminds us. The world of these poems is starlit. It swirls and shatters and becomes." —Dennis James Sweeney, author of *In the Antarctic Circle*

"There is a pulse in every line that Haviland lays onto the page, a rhythm that threads together so naturally the inward and outward, the ordinary and extraordinary. This connectedness grounds us through each exploration of humanity that Haviland poses, poems asking us again and again how to be and how to continue being in spite of everything." —Zoe Reay-Ellers

"The poems in Sam Haviland's *Lost Things* take the reader on far-flung adventures. We start in familiar suburban settings, and end up in outer space, ancient Greece, or the underworld, with pauses for reflections on evolution, geology, time, and the 'infinite me's / between today and tomorrow.' We become cyborgs, meet 'Dionysus at a Music Festival in Vermont,' and accompany two teenagers and a skeleton named Cal through the dark corridors of a locked school building at night. This intelligent, inventive, witty first collection promises many more invigorating excursions with Sam Haviland in the future."
—Melissa Monroe, author of *Medusa Beach*

"While the eye that Haviland's poems turn to the public world often wears a veneer of indexical expertise rife with defamiliarization's humorous gaps, the domestic and private poems in this collection pull the inverse maneuver, feigning exasperation at the endless self-maintenance and senseless accumulation while at their core possessing a seemingly unshakable, bottomless wisdom."
—Joe Sacksteder, author of *Make/Shift*

SAM BLYSSE HAVILAND

LOST THINGS

Moon Press
Princeton, New Jersey

Copyright © 2023 Sam Blysse Haviland
ISBN 978-1-312-81112-6
All rights reserved.

Cover art by Nicholas Bonifas

Moon Press
Princeton NJ, 08544
https://www.moonpress.org/

CONTENTS

Pineapples in December

1

Everything to Know About Man(or Wo-Man): An Index

3

Under the Influence of Evolution

6

Comet as Paper Boy

7

The Body as a Place for Lost Things

8

The End of Winter Semester

10

Crop Circles on the Boulevard

11

Everything Reminds Me of Jenga

12

TIME: Three Interpretations

14

California Walnuts

15

Snowball Earth

17

I Want to Know Legacy

18

Dionysus at a Music Festival in Vermont

19

Suburbia Burns Bright

22

What Happens When Children Erode

24

Bringing the Ground Home

26

———————

Teresa's Fantastic Haunting

27

To my family

To everyone who helped make me who I am today, and to everyone that will help make me who I am tomorrow

LOST THINGS

Pineapples in December

In the winter when my lips are chapped
I suck them into my mouth and bite off

the skin. Then I fill a bowl from the cafeteria
with pineapple and eat it out in the snow.

My ass gets wet and cold. The fruit soaks
into my gums. After, I bury my face

in the ground, and inhale snow
to help wash away the acidity. In war,

meteorologists help the army decide when
to attack—I guess the phrase rain or shine

is more complicated when the stakes are dead
bodies on New Year's. I go back

to the cafeteria and drink five cups
of coffee. I am not tired. Or I am

not tired in the way one is usually tired.
The pineapple wasn't fresh, but it's December—

what do I expect? I fill the coffee with more sugar
and cream than my friends deem acceptable

but they are busy fighting their own battles
with algebra teachers and boys and drug

store iPhone chargers. They left me
to hold down the fort. Later, when my mouth

starts to bleed, I balance ice cubes
on my tongue and let them drop into

the sink. My laptop is open, propped up
on the toilet seat. There is a coloring book,

ramen, and a 13-ounce tub of Vaseline
in my Amazon cart. I am preparing

for a siege. I stare at the weather app on my phone
hoping when the snow stops, my friends

might come back. The walls of my mouth bend
around the ice. The cold is just starting.

Everything to Know About Man(or Wo-Man): An Index

Chapter 1: Signs of Homosapien Distress

Solitude

>as pack animals they tend
>to move in groups of two
>or more. They might
>not always be in distress,
>but if you come across
>a lonely man, be on
>the lookout for these
>additional signs

Stagnation

>even when standing still,
>their body must circulate
>materials in order to keep
>faculties alive. If one has
>been immobile too long,
>press your vibratory sensors
>to their chest and feel the *pulse*
>—colloquially referred to as a *beat*

Hemorrhaging

>iron-bound, blood is red and
>related to the circulation
>mentioned previously. We don't
>want to see it, it's supposed
>to stay inside. Sometimes blood
>comes from piercing the skin
>other times it is coughed
>up or excreted.

Chapter 2: Slang

Note that colloquial vernacular shifts depending on geographic location, age, familial origin, economic status, medium of communication, and epoch

NP, used to denote language usually deemed as unprofessional. A fair amount of slang falls under this category.

Ain't_{NP}

    a contraction of the following: is not, are not, am not, has not, and have not. Interpret meaning based on context. Example: *Ain't no rest for the wicked.* For pronunciation, remember taint and faint.

Dub_{NP}

    synonymous to success or win or conquer. Used often in reference to athletics but not exclusively. Example: *ez dub guys.* In this example, the speaker has shortened easy to *ez.* This shortening is common via *text.*

Yeah

    yes. Which generally means to agree with what was just said. In trials done, yeah is seen as less hostile. The soft 'ah' must chafe their ears less, than the 'es,' though no one's sure how. Human ears are still a mystery to us.

Chapter 3: Leisure Activities

*These activities are soothing but often unproductive—at least in a quantitative sense.

Sun Bathing

    while their own biological experts
    have warned them about the harm
    rays from their local star
    may cause, many insist on lying
    under them for hours on end.
    Slathered in synthetic creams
    or protective oils, they *bake*
    —often near water.

Listening to Music

    used at times to stimulate
    the brain during transitional
    periods, many people purposefully
    designate time for the consumption
    of these curious sequences of pitched
    waves. The noises often provoke
    feelings from the listener.
    Though not all are swayed.

Wandering

    moving indefinitely with no destination
    in sight. They are not lost,
    because there is no obligation to be
    anywhere. Sometimes searching,
    sometimes in exile—by others
    or by the self. There is a spectrum.
    Wandering can last till death,
    or simply be a reprieve.

Under the Influence of Evolution

I bought you a cactus at CVS and three weeks later
you made me stand in the outdoor gardening section
of Home Depot. I cursed the sun and balanced
on the edge of the cart. You want to go stargazing

and I tell you that the sun *is* a star. You hate
when I speak in technicalities. You want me
to use words more fluidly, to abandon the subjective.
You lose my brother's bong. I don't care—

because you still lose. Isn't that fluid,
isn't that something. Bring me coffee and we can
debate all day about nothing, still smelling
of mulch and weed killer and weed, plants

and dirt. Nitrous acid in my coffee, or is that
espresso. We are the last things, but will not be
the last thing. Evolution has not finished with us
—just look at the vestigial tail they dug out

of your back before lacrosse season. And the skull
the scientists found in that well. Not human, but close to.
At home, you mix drinks, and Bloody Marys spill
down the hatch before noon. Eat your eggs

with salt, but what came first? The chicken?
The nest? You or me? I guess the sun came first,
but time is not linear so it doesn't *really* matter.
In the end, we are all just broken skulls, blooming.

Comet as Paperboy

He packs a lunch of phosphorus and amino acids
and enough water to cool a dwarf star. Overworked

and underpaid, he crash lands on an insignificant rock.
The heat from the nearest star thaws out his frozen meal

which he garnishes with iron from the planet's core.
The home office calls him and asks why he has taken

his lunch break so early. Comet as paperboy tells
the home office to fuck off. The next day more comets join him,

each one carrying a TV dinner that he helps them bring to life;
the shelves fill with meatloaf and lasagna. Home office calls again.

*What's this? You've formed a union now? Well, what
are your demands?* Comet as paperboy hangs up. They burn

their phones in the lava pits, sulfur smoke sits in the air.
The stars shine brighter with jealousy, with bitterness—

they can get their news the old-fashioned way from now on,
the comets decide. They can wait for the light to reach them.

The Body as a Place for Lost Things

After Donna J. Haraway's "A Cyborg Manifesto"

I want the word *Cyborg* tattooed
on my body. Stripped like a screw
—maybe that's why I shave

my head. Why I tug my ears
down and get the razor as close
to the skin as possible. I'll notice

the next day in class if I've missed
anything. I'll pull at the strands,
first 'cause I'm bored but then just because

they're there and they shouldn't be. Right now
there's a dinosaur on my thigh, a thin
black outline, a window for an array

of different-sized gears. The merging
of organism and machine—I want a rook
on my ribcage and a lion

on my breastplate, I want to look
like your common junk
drawer. Maybe a pack of double-A batteries

will climb up my neck, and pennies,
and dimes, a hair tie I will never use.
There's a corkscrew and a bottle opener

and I wonder how much liquor it takes
to loosen a robot's tongue, to pixelate their screen,
jam their keys. Keys are also in the drawer—

tattooed on the webbing between my fingers,
they clang together when I make a fist. I always
forget which one is for the house

and which one I found in the dirt outside.
Both are lined with rust. Sharpies and magnets
and my older brother's fake ID. 5' 6"

and his eyes are blue, but I don't want
any color. Nothing but my natural red hue
and the bulging purple veins. There's a baseball

from a Mets game. A collection of two-dollar bills.
And for some reason, I'm programmed to think
they're worth more than the bank says.

Superman lighters, and coupons,
and Christmas cards from relatives
that we don't like. Half-empty printer ink cartridges

leaking down my ankle. I've been typing
since I was eight. Pressing, clicking, clacking. One day
I'll end up in a junkyard, maybe in the junk ocean,

maybe beached. Find me with a metal
detector, sea glass pushing up into my jaw.
C Y B O R G written across my forehead.

Recognize me, fingerprints rubbed raw
by ocean salt, genetic code tangled, my double helix
vaulted into a fisherman's net. Trace the gears

—find the key between my left thumb
and pointer, it belongs to the wind-up toy
on the back of my heel that's been cut

by the waves. Circuits splayed. Turn it
and watch everything here start to breathe.

The End of Winter Semester

I like calendars but can never remember
    what day it is. I get caught up in the sun
        and the way we wrap around it. My friends

    like to argue about time and money. One thinks
        neither exists, the other is only convinced
            of money. We should bargain, the first says

and I ask if we could bargain for more time.
    We break icicles from cabin rooftops and sword fight
        in the middle of the street— *Throw it like a javelin*!

    Our track coach was never certified for that event,
        the spear hit the ground and split
            in two. The friend who believes

in money also thinks the world is flat.
    Flat but layered, like a cake. Which layer
        are we on? My friend says *the boring one.*

    What I like most about the calendar
        is the way time snakes across the page—
            I can see when winter starts, when Caesar dies,

when my friends and I will hop on planes and weeks will disappear
    behind wreathed doorways. I like the perfect square boxes.
        7 in a row. Just like there are infinite numbers

    between 0 and 1, there are infinite me's
        between today and tomorrow. We buy our time
            with a lighter and cannolis from the bakery

while watching the sun set on our layered cake, casting jagged,
    stair-step shadows. If time is not linear
        deadlines are more like circles. Never-ending

    and irrational. I like to think of the world as a pie.

Crop Circles on the Boulevard

*I walk a lonely road. The only road that I have
ever known.* I skipped the song, then the next,
hand braced against my hip as I tipped the edge
of the phone out of my pocket, thumb swiping

        down, until I heard different, less somber chords.
        The park was supposed to be ominous, but not
        depressing. A place I went when I wanted to live
        in an open container. A sparse collection of trees

gathered like mold in the corner of the plastic
Tupperware, a jungle gym like folded spaghetti
—and the long field between the two, with a tall
fence to mark the home plate of a could-have-been

        baseball pitch. I meandered around the outside
        of the green for a while, following the tar-made
        trail. It cracked in random places, and at the tops
        of hills. The benches on the side surrounded

by cigarette butts. I refused to sit on them
and instead infiltrated the grass, while something
fast and loud burst out of my back pocket
dimmed slightly by the denim. I laid down,

        eyes turned up toward the stars, or what should
        have been stars, but it was a black mass, like staring
        at the underside of an ice cream sandwich. The sleek
        body clashing with the black-blue sky. My eccentric

            English aunt has an obsidian tea set that cost
            more than her husband's last liver transplant.
            They drink gin from the china, imported from
            some third-world eruption. This black mass—

        an off-world saucer, descending upon me. The wet
        ground against my back, pushing me to meet it.

Everything reminds me of Jenga.
A dorm room looks
like a plaything. Like a block

with curved edges. I lie
on my back in the bathroom
and stare at the bottom

of my sink. At the zip ties
holding the pipes together
between the porcelain

and the wall. I've been trying
to be more honest—or maybe
open is the right word. Staring

at the bottom of the sink
helps. So does testing all the outlets
and realizing only half of them

work. At home my dad
would rip down the walls
and mess with the wires himself

or whatever you're supposed to do
when things stop holding a charge.
My desk looks like a frying pan

covered in scratches—I hang
collages above my bed,
and a calendar that doesn't start

for another four months. I stick
post-it-notes to the wall. *Laundry,
homework, buy more Cheetos.*

My roommate's shampoo bottle
falls and hits my foot in the shower,
now there's a bruise that feels

like pins and needles when I run
my hand across it. There are stacks
of playing cards and tarot cards,

I read fortunes while waiting
for the new year and count the books
on my shelf that I'll never finish.

TIME: THREE INTERPRETATIONS

ONE
I picture the red
        I picture a dotted line
I picture scissors cutting
        through my week, splitting
days in half. Half good,
        half bad. Half here, half not.
Time is porous—it bubbles
        to the surface, setting like ash
—but there are gaps.

TWO
Summers in pages,
in paper cuts, in salted
slugs. Summers in notes
on doorsteps. Summers
in sweat, in bright red
skin, in phone calls
where we say *I miss
everything* but you.

THREE
Skeletons in closets.
Skeletons dressed in suits.
My skeleton is alive and kicking

        knocking on my door, leaving
        letters, asking for money
        and sometimes just asking

for the time. Asking for me to read
a clock. And that's always when
I refuse to answer.

California Walnuts

When I was a kid I used to pull
fire alarms every chance I got.
One day, there was a track meet

that I really didn't want to go to
and I'd already thrown up a bunch
of walnuts during gym class

—had been snacking on them
all morning. You'd brought them
back from California, the fancy kind

and when you asked me where
I got them, I lied. *Home. My uncle.* Really
it was the front zipper pocket

of your red JanSport—but I bit
the bullet later, in the trash can
in the locker room, then showered

through the rest of the day, fingers
pruning, as I continued spitting
up bile, watching it slide into the drain.

I left in time to see the line of blue
and gray jerseys waiting next
to the bus. Shaking water out of my ear,

I thought, *fuck it.* And turned
to the nearest wall. By then I was used
to the blaring and I kept my head

down, shoulders hunched. Outside
you were in your uniform
smiling, face tilting, hands shoved

into gray sweats. It was like that
time you caught me cheating on
that Algebra test and pulled your paper away.

Payback for when I left you
and your brother to walk home
in the rain. Got in the car

and told my mom to book it
and you flipped me off
through the back window.

You knew that I ate your walnuts,
but you also knew I'd always
be my own deserter.

Snowball Earth

Everyone talks about Pangea but no one
    knows Rodinia, hailed the motherland   barren

as she was, a cracked desert, ozone   bleeding
    through atmosphere, like watching a pen

explode in water, Rodinia was just rock
    and they should've named *her*   after

Gaea, a face in the muddy ground   Magma
    boiling underneath her brow

Ice grows like calluses, not-dead things
pile up and earth is just a morgue   in winter

I Want to Know Legacy

There are flowers in my head—
and there are mosquitos in my ears

    —a breeze against my back
    —see I'm trying my hardest

not to care. Then I hurl my body
at the road and feel alive,

    all by accident I might add.
    Like an old World War One

fighter plane, everything
here is manual. A relative

    of mine engineered them.
    Put his mind to work

with greased propellers—
guns strapped to wings. I think a lot

    about family these days. About the clicking
    of genes, on and off, about

the symmetry of brains, and blue
blue eyes. I cover the bites

    on my skin with peppermint
    essential oil. I call my father

—then I sleep

Dionysus at a Music Festival in Vermont

The mysterious stranger talks all night.
Empties his barrels of drink for the crowd
that's gathered around his tent. They lean
as they listen, with watering mouths—

I died once. I died a couple of times.
Don't ask me what it was like. I don't
remember and it's not very important.
What's important is this stand I have,

The Best from the Vine, we've got stickers
and tote bags, they're very overpriced
don't buy them. Here, drink. It's a free
sample. Yes, the whole glass is a free sample.

Why? To spite the gods or, well, a god—
one specific goddess I mean. Also, why not?
Why question a free gift? Just enjoy it!
The Dolphins? They do look a bit out

of place next to the cheese and crackers,
don't they. They're a passion project
of mine. Porcelain? I'm not sure. No,
I'm not a sculptor, more a collector.

Usually, these venues smell of cheap beer,
powdered sugar, and incense. Tonight
the stranger has draped aristocracy over
all their vices. Pulled from the Vineyard,

from a backpacking trip in Europe,
from a New England boarding school.
Women's sandals, shiny hair, a white
flowy shirt. He hands a girl five hundred

dollars and tells her to go buy tacos. He leaves
to get more wine and returns with a goat
wearing a South Hamptons sweatshirt
and calls him an old friend. Languid sounds

drift from the speakers, a guitarist with big hair
sings about love and family and the stranger
starts to weep. Chiseled tears shine off
his chin, the whole crowd stills—

don't stop on my account, he says,
*don't do anything on my account. I've had enough
of cults. Drink your wine, eat your food. Death
is more common than you think.* He stands

on his table and kicks down
a barrel of wine, it spills a river
into the piss-soaked grass where it mirrors
the red dusk. Other vendors yell, the speakers'

feedback something vile. The woman
selling crystals throws her geodes into the Styx
where they mingle with dreams and chalupa
wrappers. A family of four with kayaks

strapped to the hood of their car paddle downstream.
People have started to fuck in the fields, even
on stage, moaning into microphones. The stranger
grins from his tent, sitting atop the fold-

out table next to plates of cheese and rows
and rows of ceramic dolphins. There is a bowl
of grapes in his lap. He eats in leisure, the river
spraying his ankles. While the goat chews through

a copy of *The Tempest.* A breeze knocks *The Best
from the Vine* stickers off his table and
into the wind, like leaves in autumn. He blows
smoke and with lidded eyes begins to speak.

*This is human. I was once human. It only
makes sense. This frenzy. This madness. I told you
that I died, right? I am not a planter, just a pruner,
making sure the fruit grows—cutting away your inhibitions.*

A group of roadies arms themselves with jagged
crystals and antique knives, they traverse
the wine rushing fields, they watch kayaks capsize.
They zero in on the strange stranger. On his

sculpted features. *Daddy's money,* the roadies whisper.
Their boots dig into mud and they surround him
like dogs, like he is weak prey. The Porta-Potties
collapse in the background as the stranger pops

another grape into his mouth. They can hear
those new-age sirens coming closer. The blue
and red blaring ones, the ones everyone
runs from. The stranger remembers other sirens

—with voices people could never turn
away from. The roadies hold up their weapons
and then disappear, leaving only a pride
of ceramic dolphins in their wake. The stranger

laughs and lays back on his table. *Hell is empty,*
he says, *and all the devils are here.*
*That's Shakespeare for you. How I love
the theater. Another form of human debauchery.*

Suburbia Burns Bright

My friends and I live
    in old houses. Old houses with peeling rooftops

and in the summer, we sit on them
    after dark. Sunburns shrivel and fall away in the wind. We pass

around a travel-sized bottle
    of aloe vera. Our feet kicking up black bits of asphalt

—sometimes whole shingles slide down
    into the side yard, into the garden, the driveway,

the back patio. We used to stargaze, but the sky
    is so polluted now. My friends and I live in old houses

and none of the doors lock. The paint
    is chipped. Stairs creak, voices drift through hollow walls

and warmth is not what it used to be—
    we were sitting on the roof when the house on Halstead

burned. Like a bruised peach or a funeral
    pyre. It was raining but the fire didn't care. When it rains we sit

in our basements. Some of them are refurbished
    but we don't like those. They're too mundane. Beige rugs

and our fathers' ellipticals in the corner. We like
    basements with pipes unveiled, with shaking machines

and a garage that smells like pennies and soil
    and sawdust. We like old houses with ancient backyards

with well pumps and birdbaths. Yellow tulips. We burn
    old furniture in an old fire pit, watch aluminum handles melt

into the grass. The house on Halstead had crown
    molding and a knocker shaped like a lion that melted and left

a puddle on the owners' welcome rug. *Home*
    SWEET Home. Old houses. Old gimmicks. Dry humor

makes dry kindling, and the wood burns
    like my skin. Like my friends' skin. Red, angry, in the dark

ash flies away with the breeze. We all smelled
    the smoke, my friends and I. And we remembered that old houses

burn quickly. That wood cracks and flames spread
    and that the hallways are much too narrow for our brackish bodies.

What Happens When Children Erode

—you know you've hit rock bottom
as a kid when your mom burns
your stamp collection and you think

> well, that's just money down the drain.
> Did you ever pick shiny bits of mica
> off the bottom of your rocks? I left

piles all around my house, on desks,
in the bathtub, in the cupholders
of the family car. Did you crack open

> your head or your chin? Seven stitches
> or thirteen? I threw myself into riptides
> swallowed sand and stayed up late

reading books about continents
covered in ice, with molten rock brewing
underneath them—about igneous and

> metamorphic. I learned my insides
> are sedimentary. Just the smushed remains
> of everything; sand, meatloaf,

cherry coke, and stamps that refused
to unstick from my tongue. In kindergarten,
we made paper and dyed scarves

> with the sun. Outlining the things we loved
> with bleach. Back then I loved stamps
> and rocks and quarters. We laid it all out

in the parking lot and I waited
with my head resting on a speed bump.
My scarf was an array of squares

    and circles and indecipherable globs—
    not a single head or tail, no striations,
    no special edition endangered animals,

not a face in sight.

Bringing the Ground Home

I met sand this afternoon,
found it pressed to my cheek
found it under my fingernails.

I met sand this evening,
left early from dinner to meet her
at the lake shore. Where the sun

was setting fast, like a boat leaving
shore. I think I'm in love with sand—
it's only been three weeks

but really I think, I've just never
felt this way about anything
—one. I mean. Anyone. I lie

awake thinking about sand.
About feeling it between my toes,
and the way it holds up my neck

the way it clings.

TERESA'S FANTASTIC HAUNTING

Teresa and I Break Curfew

There's a skeleton on the roof. Not a real one.
      We found it in the biology classroom

on the first floor, while climbing
      through the window. It fell off the shelf
onto Teresa—

she didn't even flinch. Only rested it gently
      on a desk then leaned down

to pick up the displaced phalanges
      and metacarpals. Tiny phalanxes pinging
against the linoleum.

We named him Cal, short for Calcium,
      and declared him a *he*,

after a long and heated debate:
      We're really naming him after big dairy?
I bet your bones

would snap like twigs. We heard footsteps
      and ducked. Teresa and I took cover

under the teacher's desk.
      The others scattered throughout,
Jimmying into cupboards

and praying in dark corners. The footsteps paused
      in front of the door. Teresa's breath

smelled like sour candy. It was one
      of those moments where I thought the world
would end

but I didn't mind. Then the footsteps left.
      Teresa and I stood, the plastic

bones slipping
 from her hands and spilling
between us.

Life Sciences: The Human Skeleton

I felt my ribs rattle. The curve   of a hooded shoulder
Echoed through me. *Cal,* they said, but I'm not
calcium. I'm polyethylene. I'm resin.   I'm their recycled
rubber bath toys—because of course, this school had to be
environmentally conscious.

I'm not even my own.

I've learned   enough about reactions sitting
in the back of that classroom. Enough   to know
I don't have any. No   enzymes. No   proteins. No air
flowing in and out. Except for that day, they stuck
balloons into my chest   and pricked them—

POP!

—the holes in my skull caught the light   glinting
off the lockers, but I lost it   again in the rifts
around my joints: dark as ever. I saw the two of them,
spinning   my bones like coins, like pennies and dimes
running between their knuckles.

Who's got the keys?

We left the locker-lined halls for a stairwell
with concrete steps. There was no light   here either,
but I glimpsed the gray   before the door closed behind us
and then again when another one opened.
We stumbled onto the roof. They laid me down.

I'd never seen stars before.

Teresa, Peter Parker, Cal, and myself

Our backpacks were full of chalk
        stolen from the wood sheds

behind the elementary schools.
        Those buildings are all rot
anyway and the chalk

hasn't been touched in years. The stifled
        creativity of the youth

—the plastic containers
        are filled with spiders and ants.
We cut our hands on the sharp

corners and Teresa pulls out
        a first aid kit. *Dumbasses.*

CVS brand hand sanitizer
        stings less than the official kind.
Probably means it kills less too.

Another girl, whose name is
        not important, rations out

her keychain-sized, pumpkin spice
        infused Purell. I decline, that stuff gives
me hives. Teresa's is scentless

and there's more of it, so it stings less
        until I soak my hands.

Then cover each wound
        with a breathable, Spiderman
band aid. Teresa's knelt down

next to Cal, gripping chalk. She draws him
        a pillow, then a sword.

Life Sciences: Adaptations

They never brought me down, and then I saw
the biggest star. The sun rising   over the horizon
—they don't talk much   about stars in biology—
rumor is   that it's just a ball of gas. But ecology
says it's important. I know   about the sun.

The source of all energy.

I thought lying   there would bring me to life,
but it didn't, and I was stuck. With a flat pink sword
under my left ulna.   I thought they weren't coming back.
But they did,   after the sun went down and up
three more times.

All the while I felt something growing beneath me.

Loud, filling,   getting ready to burst. Cytolysis,
when osmosis gets overloaded, and the cells—*POP*
—then they opened the door   and stormed
out, feet pounding   like a herd. The same girl
sat next to me.

All reactions require energy.

This girl is some sort of spark, breaking bonds
like phosphorus.   She carries matches in her back pocket
and a deck of cards. She took my hands, then gave
me a weapon. Does she know I watched her fail
that test six months ago?   From the back corner.

The catalyst.

Night Shift Secretary: Audio Log One

Principal Jensen says he doesn't need a night shift,
but I disagree. Someone's got to keep the ghouls
from messing with things.

It's not your job.
Well, then what is my job?

Fine do what you want,
just don't let the superintendent

know about it. Secretaries these days,
they think they own the place. I blame sitcoms

It's probably better this is off the books anyway—
Then the ghouls wouldn't listen. Money invalidates things.
Money skews time and dream.

That's what they say.
Dream. I haven't dreamed

since I met them. Haven't slept
either. Just curl on my side

breathing in lemon-scented
floor wax.

And I've been piling up my checks from the day shift in a locker
down corridor F. The one with the dinged, dark red combination lock.
7, 12, 32. Mostly I just push them through the slits.

All that money. I'm not sure
what would happen if I opened it.

Teresa and I do the dirty work then she disappears

The stairway is covered in chalky
        handprints that Teresa and I spend

an hour cleaning up. They others
        left early, giggling all the way
down. The flashlights

on our phones were too bright
        so we use the light from the home

screens. Three notifications
        from mom, five from dad,
and my favorite podcast,

21st Century Oracle, just released
        a new episode: *The Underworld Wants*

You! We don't have water
        or rags so we wash the concrete
walls with hand sanitizer

and the dark-colored sweatshirts
        we wore to try and blend

with the shadows.
        We don't seem to need
them now, even Teresa's

bright yellow Converse are just
        sound. The dull thump of soles.

She turns around
        the bend of the stairwell
her phone lighting

up the scratches on the wall.
        Then it's dark. Then a door opens and shuts.

Night Shift Secretary: Audio Log Two

I'm not superstitious. I always thought religion was for quacks.
Then the ghouls turned the shadows into ducks and I shoved
a whole loaf of bread into the gymnasium wall.

A week's worth of sandwiches
bought me the void

whispering in my ear. Keeping
time, like a metronome

but only sounding like a bomb.
They say the whole place

is about to give and the kids on the roof aren't helping. The ghouls
watched them snatch the key from Jensen's desk. I just watch
their shoes scuff the floor.

It's like standing on bubble
gum, either the bubble pops

or something sinks and the membrane
wraps around. Engulfing.

The ghouls want
the girl.

I told them to swallow her
like they did the bread—
they said that's not how this works.

21st Century Oracle: The Underworld Wants You!!!!

Sounds of water rushing, stones hitting each other. It slowly merges with techno music. A soothing but raucous sound. At the end, someone hits a gong.

Enter the 21st century:

I met a lady while buying a train ticket in Grand Central. She handed me a bundle of envelopes.

Told me that if I took them time would stand still again. I told her I had an appointment.

Appointment: noun, an arrangement to meet someone at a particular time and place

Then she started talking to me about particles. Subatomic, anatomic. Electrons and organelles.

She was wearing a blue/red ski jacket over a beige cardigan, her shoes flat, her hair in a bun—

I told her again, I have an appointment. She started shaking her head, holding the envelopes out.

7, 12, 32. There's a school a couple stops away from here. In Westchester. About to go under.

Westchester? Those rich motherfuckers? What happened? Don McLean come rolling into town?

Did the music die again? Then the lady specified. *A different kind of under.* Then she got vague.

Something dark and cavernous. Something without hands. Something asking for her hands.

I wanted to tell her to take a hike but she pointed at the ceiling and I watched the constellations.

It's like in video games, when the boat sails across the map. The pegasus rammed into Orion.

The blue folded over into something else. The lady grabbed my arm and pulled. Stronger than

she looks. She pulled until we were at the tracks, shadows pooling between the grates. No rats,

no dirt, no nothing. She wanted me to jump. I told her to go to hell. Sure, she said.

Teresa's Snap Story

Close up of Cal
    his hands are folded on top of his stomach
    he's wearing a West Lake Baseball sweatshirt—#23
    the caption reads "he needs pants"

Black Square
    just black
    the caption reads "ghouls don't believe in pants, what about skirts"

Plastic Bones
    hands covered in Spiderman band-aids hold the plastic hand bones
    chalk smeared Converse can be seen below the hands
    there is no caption

Hands
    a photo of the stairwell, the flash on
    a dozen chalky hand prints, one wrapped around the metal bannister
    the photo seems washed out, the edges darker than they should be
    the caption reads "assholes, it's like they want us to get caught"

Red Combo Lock
    the caption reads "7. 12. 32."

Envelopes
    the locker is open with envelopes piled up inside and out
    the caption reads "wtf"

Black Square pt. 2
    the caption reads "i should probably delete all this, the ghouls want me to"

Stars
    the night sky, speckled
    there is no caption

TWO JOURNEYS TO THE UNDERWORLD

Teresa part I

The way to the underworld is by train,
a train that pulls up halfway down
D Corridor, between Mr. Smith and Ms. Carlucci's
classrooms. It pulls up, steam and smoke pooling
on the floor, shifting to fill the empty bodies of ghouls.
Making the unseen seen

        The way to the underworld is not like the myth,
no river of dreams, just a gray and blue bullet stretched
      to fit a frame. Transcontinental: made to bust through plates of
granite.

Surrounded by nothing but steam,
Teresa feels the mist first in her hair.

The Secretary I

It wasn't as dramatic as jumping onto tracks,
The secretary is not sure if fortune-telling is inherently
theatrical or if this is a product of the media

—phones forcing producers to taint every simple thing.
Not that this is simple. Not that it's complicated.
All she did was board. Purse clutched to her chest,

ticket in hand, ghouls parting to let her through
the aisle. Though it felt rather simple. As simple as death
could be. Is she dead?

Questions are simple. And she really doesn't care for the answers.

Teresa part II

Stepping on board, her hair relaxes,
frizz fading back to how it was before,
before she even left the house that morning.
Like the impression of the world is just gone—
but the ghouls are still with her, their steam less corporeal
more ethereal. She can sense straight backs,
and curved spines.

    Life is a mixture of people with good and bad posture,
She supposes death is the same. She pictures
  a skeleton relaxing, its spine rolling out

after the soul leaves the body,
nothing there to draw the tension.

The Secretary part II

It's late winter, and everyone has been in the mood
to get sick. So her purse was half office supplies
half cough drops. She felt like a drug dealer at times,

Popping open her desk drawer, beckoning people close
but not too close. It was a miracle she hadn't caught
whatever was going around.

Now she can feel herself losing her voice
but she doesn't think a cough drop will help. Her voice
is getting lost in the literal way,

having trouble finding the path home,
it thinks it belongs to the hiss of the tracks,
the rush of the wind, the gears of the train

clicking and churning.

Teresa part III

Teresa had never gotten out much, fifteen
and the world felt terribly small, same people,
same places. That school that she'd grown up in
—D Corridor vanishes behind her,
she sits now, thinking that it's nice to be going
someplace:

    not thinking about what's being left, who's being left.
The world is terribly small. Trains often run
  through the same place twice.

She's sure she'll run
into them again

The Secretary part III

She spent a lot of time on trains as a kid,
and she always preferred the journey to the destination.
She preferred windows, she preferred observing,

out the window now she sees glimpses of everything
she's ever seen before and also things she hasn't.
She remembers being told a lot that life is about

experiences. Collecting them, cherishing, being—
just being—in them. Now she's not sure how to feel.
Not sure if she bought a one-way ticket

or round trip. For the first time in her life
or death, she feels there's more inside than out,
her brain swirling

shaping a world behind her eyes.
Suddenly the ghouls seem like jellyfish—bloated
and unbothered. And she is just being.

On a train. Underground. The opposite of everything.

Teresa's gone, it's just me

Linoleum, cement, the sunken in rooftop
        where every step *squelches—*

I retraced our steps, then came back
        here. It's three-fifty. I should leave
soon. Cal hasn't moved,

        he's the only thing that never moves,
his bones white in the dark,

        like staring into an open mouth.
I think about taking him with me,
        a piece of him at least.

But this feels kind of like a funeral,
        and what kind of mourner

would I be, shoving pieces of the deceased
        into my pocket. Hand gripping
his skull like a bowling ball.

        Death is less about taking and more
about leaving. Flowers, clothes, jewelry,

        tombs filled to the brim with gold
and silver. But me. I don't think I have much
        to give.

Life Sciences: The Life Cycle & Prey/Predator roles (Cal's Farewell)

Years ago they wrapped me in clay.

To simulate   the layers of the skin. Three types
of dermis. They stretched it too tight,   and I looked
starved. Now   they're shoving a shirt over my head,
carefully pulling my arms   through the sides. Polyester
over polyethylene.

Is this what it means to peak in high school?

In a couple of months, after rain and snow, at the beginning
of spring—mold will start to grow. I'll feel it   building up
behind my eye sockets, like a tension headache. Until a hawk
flies off with my skull, and the cardinals and sparrows
pick at the smaller things.

Becoming a part of the ecosystem.

The sword at my side is no good,   melting in the morning
mist. I'll still remember the girl   who gave it to me. Who took
my hands. Who brought me   here. Even while soaring,
talons digging into   the softened plastic. How she handled
my bones like poker chips.

I felt like a bet or a bluff. Still do sometimes.

At least the school didn't implode. She left and the place
calmed down. Or maybe it wasn't her   leaving. I can't
figure it out. That other kid came back alone and pressed
a bandaid   into my sternum. Peeled it off their hand
and left it there.

Acknowledgements

Poems in this collection have previously appeared in *Blue Marble Review, Okay Donkey, Ninth Letter Web Issue, figments,* and *Nassau Literary Review.*

There are a lot of people that helped make this book what it is; books are like people in that way. Filled to the brim with the influence of others. I'll try my best to thank as many people as I possibly can, but it feels like a task I'm doomed to fail.

I would like to start by thanking my readers. And I'm starting first with that because it'll apply to everyone that picks up this book, not just the people that had a hand in its creation, but the strangers and the friends of friends. I'd like to thank you for being willing to try something new. And to the other readers, the ones who know me, the ones who love me, the ones who merely find me an interesting/worthy addition to their daily life, the ones who want to know me better—thanks for taking the chance to get to know this other part of me.

Now into the nitty gritty details that you're welcome to skim or overlook altogether. Forewarning, in my writing I've always been told I use more words than necessary to get my point across:

First, I'll thank my family—my brother and my parents, fully showing my appreciation for them is an impossible task, but also if it wasn't for them and their unyielding support I probably would never have met all the other people I'll be thanking next. One of the most important things my parents did was let me go to this boarding school in Northern Michigan; Interlochen Arts Academy, where I spent three years studying creative writing in all its wonderful and mind-blowing forms.

From here I'd like to thank all the wonderful people I met at Interlochen. Joe Sacksteder, Bri Cavallaro, and Mika Perrine—three wonderful mentors of mine. Bri the poetry teacher that first got me excited about something that wasn't prose. Joe being the teacher willing to indulge all my weird literary experiments. And Mika, who always had just the right story for me to read. These three were instrumental in my development as a writer. Their classes, their advice, their support, I'm sure are things I'll continue to carry with me for many more years to come. Not to mention an overwhelming amount of the poetry in this book came form Bri's class *Stories in Verse*. And the title of the collection would never have been if it wasn't for Joe introducing me to Donna J. Haraway's "A Cyborg Manifesto."

It wasn't just the teachers that shaped my experience and my writing at Interlochen, but also my peers. Zoe Reay-Ellers has always been my go-to when it comes to poetry (but she's also always willing to read anything I write, no matter the genre), for recommendations, for feedback, when I'm stuck on something, or when I just need to talk to another writer. Out of everyone in the world she probably knows my writing best. Close second to Zoe is Neva Ensminger-Holland. Neva and I began our tentative foray into the world of poetry together. They, like Zoe, are always willing to read anything I write, and have a great eye for minute details that I tend to miss. Nicholas Bonifas is an important note in this acknowledgement. He studied writing with the rest of us at Interlochen, but he's also a gifted visual artist, and I am incredibly thankful that he was willing to use his talents to help create the cover of this collection. It's incredible. He created something new and unique that still speaks to my work as a whole, and I don't think he'll give himself enough credit for it when it comes out.

There are so many other people from Interlochen, at this point it'd be easier to give you my high school yearbook than to try and name every single one of them. All the people that read my work—Morgan Spencer, Grace Schlett, and Deen Lott-Clough, to name a few. All the people that kept me sane while I was writing—special shoutout to Elizabeth Schretzmann and Emelia Ciccolini. David Tanis, for his mentorship outside of the classroom. Mary Ellen Newport for her Advanced Biology class—and for nurturing and indulging the curiosities of her students. Again there are so many other teachers and students and people who I met during my time there who influenced me and, by extension, my work. I wrote most of this collection at Interlochen, or while I was missing Interlochen. I think I miss it a little everyday, especially the people. It was the first place I was able to fully express myself the way I wanted to; partially by being such an open and welcoming place, but also by giving me the artistic tools I needed to tell the stories I wanted to tell.

Of course, Interlochen isn't my whole world, just a huge part of it so far, and there are many other significant contributors to this collection, including William Fargason, poet and editor for *Split Lip Magazine*. During the summer of 2021, I worked with him through a mentorship program run by The Young Writers Initiative; some of the stuff I wrote that summer is in this book, and the experience also really helped me start to find my voice as a poet. Everyone at Moon Press for their help during the revision process. Rosemary Dietz was especially helpful, with great feedback and stellar leadership skills when it came to organizing meetings.

Besides specific thanks, I'm just grateful that I've lived in places and times where my artistic pursuits have been encouraged. Where this book is possible.

About the Author

Samantha Blysse Haviland is from Mamaroneck, New York. Their work has previously appeared in *Okay Donkey, Ninth Letter Web Issue, Blue Marble Review, Lumiere, Wintermute,* and *The Interlochen Review.* They are currently a freshman at Princeton University studying English Literature and Creative Writing. Previously, they studied writing at Interlochen Arts Academy. They enjoy writing in all genres but are especially fond of experimental work. They also like dogs and hot chocolate, but are not averse to tea.

Moon Press is Princeton University's first student-run publishing press dedicated to empowering students through the publishing process, amplifying emerging voices, and strengthening our campus community. We publish students' longform works on a yearly cycle.

We are grateful for the support provided by:

DEPARTMENT OF ENGLISH at PRINCETON
LEWIS CENTER FOR THE ARTS at PRINCETON
PRINCETON USG

& the committed members of Moon Press:

Selena Hostetler '23
Ergene Kim '23
Elliott Hyon '24
Dori Kollar '24
JJ Scott '24
Anika Asthana '25
Annie Cao '25
Caroline Coen '25
Rosemary Dietz '25

Vera Ebong '25
Yejin Suh '25
Emily Yang '25
Audrey Zhang '25
Anne Duong '26
Melanie Garcia '26
Jeannie Kim '26
Kayla Xu '26
Sarah Zhang '26

To learn more about Moon Press, visit https://www.moonpress.org/ online and princetonmoonpress on Instagram

Writing is set in Baskerville Old Face. Heads set in Montserrat.
Cover design by Nicholas Bonifas.

CPSIA information can be obtained
at www.ICGtesting.com
Printed in the USA
BVHW042017120423
662236BV00029B/536